LESTER'S
OVERNIGHT

LESTER'S
OVERNIGHT

written and illustrated by
KAY CHORAO

E. P. Dutton & Co., Inc.   New York

· *Library of Congress Cataloging in Publication Data*

Chorao, Kay   Lester's overnight.
SUMMARY: Lester's overnight with Auntie Belle
is nothing like home.

[1. Aunts—Fiction.   2. Night—Fiction]   I. Title.
PZ7.C4463Le   [E]   76-50029   ISBN 0-525-33480-7

Published simultaneously in Canada by Clarke,
Irwin & Company Limited, Toronto and Vancouver

Editor: Ann Durell
Designer: Meri Shardin
Printed in the U.S.A.   First Edition
10 9 8 7 6 5 4 3 2 1

For my Ian David

Lester was spending his first night away from home. He was staying with Auntie Belle.

"I want to go with my mother and father," whispered Lester.

"Your parents can't take you with them,"
said Auntie Belle. "They are going to be all
tied up with your father's employer."
"Tied up?"
"Yes."

Auntie Belle's house wasn't anything like home.

For dinner, Auntie Belle served broccoli.
Three stalks sat on Lester's plate beside
his pot roast.
At home Mother made things like
hamburgers and carrot sticks.

"After dinner you must meet Tom. He's
my new tiger cat," said Auntie Belle.
"No, thank you," said Lester.

While Auntie Belle washed the dishes,
Lester looked for a place to hide from Tom.

"Oh, I see you found Tom, after all," said Auntie Belle. "But now it is time for bed, dear."

Lester climbed the stairs with Auntie
Belle.

At home there were no stairs.

"I'll help you with your bath," said Auntie
Belle.

"I can do it myself," said Lester.

But he wished his mother was there to
wash his back.

Lester took a bath with purple soap.
His mother always bought white soap.
"After your bath, put on your pajamas
like a good little lamb," said Auntie Belle.

After the hot bath, the floors felt cold on Lester's feet. At home there was carpet, warm and soft. At home there was a mother and a father.

"Get into bed, dear. Night is upon us,"
said Auntie Belle.

"Is it a good knight?"

"A very good night, Lester."

"Will you read me a story, Auntie Belle?"

At home his mother or father read to Lester every night.

"No, Lester, no stories. You should think up your own. You need more imagination."

"Good night, Auntie Belle."

"Good night, dear."

Then she kissed him and turned out the light.

Auntie Belle left the door open a crack, and Tom slipped in.

With a tiger guarding his feet and a good knight guarding his roof, Lester felt safe.

"Tomorrow I'm going to untie my mother and father," he whispered.

Then he fell asleep.

KAY CHORAO says that *Lester's Overnight* is based on two very real things in her own experience. One is the first night she spent away from home when she went to camp at the age of six. In a fit of daylight bravado, she asked for a top bunk, and then lay awake, with tears streaming silently into her ears, because she was afraid she would fall out and crack her head open, like Jack in the nursery rhyme!

The other is observations of the way her own children misinterpret words. Once when accused of "hanging around," her son said seriously, "but there aren't any handles in the ceiling."

The author of *Maudie's Umbrella* and other books, as well as illustrator of such titles as *Albert's Toothache,* Ms. Chorao lives in New York City.

The title display is Cochin Open No. 262 set in monotype. The other display and text are Goudy Old Style set in film. The art was drawn with pencil to create soft tones and the book was printed by offset at Halliday Lithographers.